Grace and the Wolf

KAT GOSS

Hylosis Publishing LLC
hylosis.pub

ISBN eBook: 9798894030326
ISBN Paperback: 9798894030333

This is a work of fiction. Names, characters, places, and incidents portrayed are the product of the author's imagination or are used fictitiously. Any resemblance to actual persons (living or deceased), establishments, events, products, or locales is entirely coincidental and unintended.

Written by humans for humans. This book may not be used to train generative AI without written consent from the publisher.

I would like to thank all who have read my work with a special gratitude—the kind that keeps me up at night and weathers all my storms. I thank those who have put their faith in me and deemed my writing suitable to be put out into the world, who have published my work and stood proudly by it.

With each clack of my keyboard, another dream comes true.

TABLE OF CONTENTS

THE CONVERSATION

NOBODY NOTICED THE WOLF. His large, furred figure crowded her field of view as he sat down across the table from her. For a brief moment, she choked. Her red wine cast a fine spray over the pristine tablecloth, leaving a shadow where the wolf's claws had rested, paw pads down as if he were comfortable there. Was the wine making her see things?

Grace glanced around, uncertain of what to feel. Was fear the appropriate response when nobody else seemed afraid? It had been stranger still when he'd opened his mouth and offered her a polite greeting.

"Are you new in town?" he asked as he perused the menu.

There was no meal on there large enough for the likes of him. When he spoke, flashes of his teeth and fangs peeked out from behind his lips. He didn't appear self-conscious of it at all. Nor did he seem concerned that he stood out rather boldly among the rest of the room.

The other patrons were largely farmers and their families. Grace was stopped at the first small town of many and wondered if they'd all be so strange.

"No," she answered. "I'm only passing through. I'm on a trip and will leave again tomorrow morning."

"You'll be staying at the guest house then," he mumbled.

There was only one place to stay in town: a quiet, dated guest house at the end of the main street. There wasn't a single item of furniture that didn't creak, as if groaning from decades of overuse.

"What are you doing here, then?" he asked, pulling his eyes from the menu and glancing at her bottle of wine.

"Would you like a glass?" she offered.

"No, no, I shouldn't," he answered. "It is terrible for my figure and turns me into such a beast. Besides, I've already had my dinner."

"Here?" she asked, looking around.

Had he been there the entire time? Had she missed him somehow?

"When morning comes, where will you be going?" he asked.

He was a nosy creature. Grace took a sip as she pondered just how much she should tell him. He leaned back, the chair bending beneath his weight, and tucked his paws behind his head.

"To Cragspire Peak," she said. "It's been on my bucket list for a while."

His amber eyes took in every detail of her small figure, and she nervously crossed her arms in front of her. The world was strange enough without talking wolves. Grace was well out of her depths.

"The Crag?" He lowered his paws from behind his head and let out a chuckle. "You don't seem like much of a hiker."

"How would you know that?" Her brows fell into their signature furrow as she spat the words out.

"I've seen many hikers here for the peak," he explained, unconcerned about her changing mood. "They're usually a little more tanned, slightly podgier, and...much more excited about it than you."

"Well, I'm not lying to you. I'm here to hike the peak," she said defiantly.

The waiter delivered her food, paying no mind to the panting thing across from her. Was she finally losing her mind? That might have been a suitable explanation, only nobody seemed to react when she spoke. Surely, if she'd been speaking out loud to something imaginary, they might have at the very least offered a concerned glance?

"I didn't mean to offend you," he said with a grin.

It was a toothy, wide grin. The kind she knew hid a large tongue and a cavernous mouth. The tip of his tail shot out over the edge of the table and quickly back again.

"It's a small town, and we don't get many new faces through here this time of year," he said. "Particularly not for the peak."

She swallowed. "Well, I would have come another time, but things aligned now, and I didn't want to miss this opportunity."

Grace felt small, like a child being called into the principal's office. The wolf gave her the same expectant look that she'd seen back then. The sort that told her she needed to explain a little more.

"I ended my marriage," she explained. "I'm here to hike this peak as a symbol of the start of something new."

"Something new?" the wolf asked. "Was it so terrible?"

"It wasn't what I wanted," she answered.

The wolf straightened out the tablecloth as she took her first bite of food. He paid her plate of steak and chips no attention as she tucked in.

"When you get back down from the peak, do you think you'll know what you want?" he asked.

She nodded through bites. "That's the plan, I guess."

He raised his brows. "It will test you."

The wolf's voice was gentler than she'd have thought. It seemed smooth and practiced, like the sort one might hear on a radio talk show. The more he spoke, the more normal it seemed. It must have been normal—nobody seemed to care about it at all.

"It will be a little cold, I suspect," she said. "But I'm determined. Besides, I haven't thought about what else I might do. This is precisely the sort of thing that will drive him mad."

"Drive who mad?"

"My husband... ex-husband," she answered.

"Ah." The wolf nodded as if he understood all the intricacies of the human world in detail. Did wolves have divorces?

There was a childlike, excited glimmer in his eyes. The more she ate, the more at ease Grace felt. The rumble in her stomach stilled, and the dizziness she'd felt upon arrival subsided. The effects of the wine were no longer so severe, either.

Even the wolf seemed a little less large and a little more like she could reach out and stroke him.

"I begged him to let me come so many times, and he always refused," Grace explained. "I was quite the adventurer before him, and I've wasted many years inside that house, pretending that admin and dinner parties would be fulfilling enough for me."

"That does sound tedious," the wolf said, bemused. "I'd have left him, too."

From somewhere in her depths, laughter arose. It bubbled up like a child who enjoyed a bad joke.

"Which route will you drive to get there?" he asked.

Blank. There was no answer to that question in Grace's mind. Until that moment, she'd focused only on getting to Crag Town. She'd assumed reaching the peak would be clear and simple. Now that he'd mentioned it, though, she was yet to see a single sign pointing her in the right direction.

"You could take the roundabout way," he continued without her answer. "It is a little less tricky in this weather, but it is a longer drive. The direct way is a rougher road. If you're not afraid of heights and a little slipping and sliding, that one should suffice."

Her confidence wavered. "I'll take the roundabout way then."

The wolf nodded. "It starts at the old mill. You'll find a four-way split in the road. Take the second from the left and then follow the path until you see the third creek. At that point, you veer to the right and keep left at splits. When the tree that looks like an elephant's trunk is to your left, you stop. That's where you'll start the hike."

Grace wished for a notebook and a pen. She remembered the first and last instructions but had lost every bit of information in between. When he was finished, he was met with her empty stare.

"It's not so complicated, but it is far," he said.

She held up her hand. "I come from the city. It's a grid network. What you just told me is like something from a pirate map. I have no idea what you're talking about and no idea where to go."

When he laughed, it was like a roar. It was guttural and seemed to echo within his throat. The wolf threw his head back, slapping his knee as he caught his breath, panting again from the laughter.

"Let me get my notebook," she said. "I can write it down."

"You could," he said with a shrug. "Or I could just come with you. I'll guide you there."

It was one thing to invite a stranger along on a drive, but a wolf with fangs and claws was another level of dangerous.

"No, thank you," she said. "I'm sure that I can manage. I'll get there eventually."

"Really, it would be no bother," he said with his syrupy voice. "I have nothing else going on and I'd rather like to see you off on this journey of yours."

He said it as if her changing her life around was a silly thing—something he didn't quite believe would happen.

"Part of this journey is figuring it out for myself," she tried again.

"If you take the wrong road, you'll wind up other side of the peak," the wolf said. "This is not the sort of place you want to get lost."

He was an insistent wolf, and Grace didn't trust him. Part of her plan was to discover things through loneliness. However, after listening to his directions, she was beginning to wonder just how naive she'd been when she'd set off.

"Don't take this the wrong way," she said, "but you're a stranger. I'm not sure how much I should trust you."

Something flashed in his eyes. She wasn't sure if it was offense or amusement.

"I suppose," he said. "You're also a stranger, and I trust you."

"I couldn't harm you if I tried," she said, taking a sip of her drink.

"Tell you what, you can think about it," the wolf said. "If you decide you need my help, you can meet me at the fuel station. If you don't show, I'll move on with my day."

"How long exactly will you wait?" she asked.

"Until I get bored, I suppose," the wolf answered with a chuckle. "I really don't have all that much going on."

It was a terrible idea, easily the worst idea yet, and she found herself more and more convinced of it the more they spoke.

"I have nothing to gain from hurting you," the wolf said. "Honestly. Have I done anything to scare you yet?"

"Well, I don't remember inviting you to join me," she said. "Yet, here you are and you're showing no signs of leaving."

He leaned forward and spoke low and quietly. "Would you like me to leave?"

She wasn't sure if it was the strangeness of the situation or her desperation for something different from her ordinary life, but she wanted him to stay.

"No," she answered. "Not really."

"Good," the wolf said. "I was hoping you'd say that."

Grace felt settled into the evening then. The wolf had a voice as soothing as a radio presenter, and she was starting to enjoy listening to him talk. She listened to stories of hikers who had seen wondrous things and others who had been trapped on the mountain for days after drinking too heavily on a camping trip.

He told each story with flair and interest, much like her grandfather had done when she was younger and he told her stories of war and history. He was so far from the sort of character she would normally spend time with that she found him somewhat enchanting.

He was smug and charming, while remaining unexpectedly relatable.

"It's settled then," the wolf eventually said. "I'll come with you for the drive. I rather look forward to the views."

She didn't recall agreeing to it, yet, but didn't argue. It seemed her plan was quickly being carried away from her. There was something thrilling about it, perhaps it was the alcohol or the general atmosphere. She couldn't be quite sure.

She nodded. "Alright. I'll be leaving at eight."

"Then I'll be waiting from seven fifteen," the wolf said with a grin.

THE DRIVE

HIS SHOULDER WAS PRESSED against the car window, the edges of his fur rippling in the current of the air conditioner. It seemed as if his knees were pressed up against his chest, despite his seat being pushed as far back as it possibly could go.

Despite many attempts to check on him, he assured Grace that he was perfectly comfortable and happy to see her again.

She'd woken up with a sense of foreboding and, when she'd glanced out the window and seen some heavy clouds, she'd been convinced that her trip would come to a sudden end. However, the clouds soon cleared, and the wolf assured her that there was no need for concern.

Grace had spent all night convincing herself that, despite her wishes to make the journey alone, some company right up until the start of the climb was perhaps not the worst idea.

"I'm glad you showed," she said, feeling rather sheepish in his presence.

"Why wouldn't I?"

She shrugged. "Not sure. I thought maybe you'd change your mind or see the weather and decide you had better things to do."

He gave her a sideways glance, and she thought she saw a smirk. As much as a giant wolf could smirk.

"I really don't have all that much going on, to be honest," he answered.

"So then what do you do?"

The wolf signalled left, and she followed his prompt just in time, slamming on the brakes to make it. Thankfully, there wasn't much traffic in a small town, so when her worried eyes checked the rear-view mirror, she saw nothing but open road and felt her shoulders ease.

"A little bit of this and that," he answered. "I sort of wake up every morning and see where the day takes me."

It didn't make much sense and wasn't much of an answer. In fact, it only posed further questions. Did a wolf need money? Was he living somewhere that required him to pay rent? After all, it was clear that it wasn't the first time he'd been in the passenger seat of a car. How exactly was he living?

The thought of him spending the night at a small restaurant in the company of others and then curling up outside somewhere to sleep didn't sit right with her.

"You'll keep going straight for some time. Make sure to enjoy the views, though. It's a pretty area," he said, turning his head to peer out of the window.

He let out a yawn, the warmth of his breath steaming up the entire window. How would she tell people she knew about what happened? How could she explain to them the wolf that had kept her company and all they'd done?

Those thoughts were soon dissolved by the landscape around them. The road was slowly starting to climb. In between the trees, she spotted glimpses of valleys and rolling mountains. Clouds dotted the blue skies as the wind tilted the tops of the trees back and forth.

"Have you always lived here?" she asked.

The wolf nodded. "Mm-hmm. Half a year at a time. Then I move on to another place for the other half of the year. It's a seasonal thing."

"I've always thought living that way made the most sense," she said. "I had an aunt who would live half the year here and the other half in Madagascar. She only ever saw summer. She often claimed she was allergic to winter."

"I'm allergic to grapes," he said matter-of-factly. "Your aunt had the right idea."

"I think I'm allergic to winter," she said. "I manage the first month or so and then I start to get really down about things."

The wolf turned his gaze back to her. "You know what you need?" he asked. "A really good fur coat. I tell you, just knowing that you have it and can pull it on and make your friends jealous will make any winter better."

Grace chuckled. "I suppose you'd know all about that."

"What sorts of things get you down in the winter?" he asked.

She exhaled. "Just about everything," she answered. "I get upset that the season for flowers is so short. All that work in creation deserves more time in the sun. It upsets me that each year, the way we order coffee seems to change. I can't keep up."

He waved right, and once again, she had to almost screech to a stop to make their turn.

"Then magazines start to bother me, you know?" she continued. "I buy them to use for reference, and all I see are advertisements. Why would I keep spending money to look at images of things I have no interest in buying? The fact that bathtubs are made out of porcelain, a substance that is so cold each winter morning. Don't even get me started on the toilet seat..."

"Humans really had the ability to design the world to be a place of comfort and truly went the wrong way," the wolf said with a huff. "It has always boggled..."

Silence fell between them there, as if he got too lazy to finish his thought. However, she had a good idea of what he might have been trying to say.

"You know, I knew a woman once who designed couches for a living," the wolf said. "She always went for straight, modern lines. There isn't a single straight line on the human body. It never made any sense to me."

Grace slammed her hand lightly on the dashboard. "Thank you!" she said. "You see? None of it makes any sense. Why would you ever need a single-cup teapot? Just brew it in the cup!"

"I think you'd be upsetting an entire community of people by saying that out loud," the wolf said with a chuckle. "But not me. I am inclined to agree with you there."

The road wound along ahead of them as they made their way to the start of The Crag. Already, the landscape was changing to something more sinister. There were trees and brush, but they were neighboured by large jutting rocks. The road turned to gravel, and she slowed.

"Not much further," he said, shifting in his seat as if to prepare himself for a bumpy ride.

She wondered if it didn't make more sense for him to run out ahead of her. Surely, he was designed for that sort of thing? Yet there he was, seated comfortably in the air conditioning.

"This man you've left behind," he said. "Was he one of the things that made you sad in the winter?"

"Absolutely," she said. "At first, I blamed the winter for it. Later, I realized it was just him."

"Huh."

The wolf reached up and scratched at his ear, his long claw reaching through the thick of his fur and touching his scalp.

"This journey is supposed to help you forget him?" he asked.

"No, I don't think I could forget him," she answered. "It is supposed to help me discover what matters most to me."

"You don't already know?" His scratching grew more violent, sending fine fur hairs into the air, decorating the front seats like canine confetti.

"I don't," she answered, somewhat ashamed of the fact. "I've never stopped to figure it out. I try to make others happy, and my own joy seems to fall to the bottom of my priorities."

"That's a shame," he said. "I know exactly what makes me happy."

"What would that be?" she asked.

The wolf sighed. "Warm sun, cool water, days to myself, and most importantly, I love to experience new things."

"I wish I could answer that question so easily," she said. "Maybe when I'm done with this."

"Why do you think you'll figure it out while on the mountain?" the wolf asked. "Surely it isn't necessary."

"What I'm hoping for is that it might be terrible," she said. "That I might feel tired and over it and, in that way, I'll know what it is that I long for."

"And what you long for will be what makes you happy?" he asked.

She spotted the sign that pointed in the direction of the hiking trail. She was minutes out and, with the wolf's company, she felt significantly less afraid.

"Yes, in theory." She slowed the car and searched for the entrance to the trail.

Knowing that in just a few minutes she would start on easily the most difficult hike of her life, her stomach twisted. Grace had anticipated regret or concern, but nervousness took her by surprise.

"I think it will work," the wolf said, and she was reminded that they were actually still in the middle of a conversation. "I think you'll find your answers here."

She smiled and felt the sense of nervousness disappear for just a moment. "Thanks."

When the wolf had sat down across from her at her table the night before, she could never have believed that they would get along so well. The entrance to the trail came into view, marked by a small, faded sign and she stopped.

"This is it," the wolf said, tapping the dashboard. "Will you be able to find your way back when you're done?"

Grace hadn't been paying nearly enough attention. She had no idea how to find her way back and hoped that perhaps there would be signs all the way back down the mountain.

"I'm glad to have met you," the wolf said as he opened the door. "I'll head back down, I guess."

He closed the door, and she sat in silence and felt frozen in place. Until the moment he'd stepped out of the car, she hadn't considered yet that they would part ways so soon. She was just starting to enjoy the conversation.

A tree, stretched out like the trunk of an elephant, loomed over the trail. The entrance to the path was dark and rough, and she stared at it for some time, imagining just how quiet it would be to take the first steps. There were no cars, no sign of anybody else on the trail. Suddenly, she felt as though she had bitten off more than she could chew.

A knock on her window made her yelp. She snapped her head to the side and was met with the large eyes of the wolf staring back at her.

"This is where you're supposed to get out," he said through the window. "Can't go on your journey from there."

She opened the door and cool air rushed in, chilling her to the bone.

"Come with me," she said, surprising herself entirely.

The wolf frowned. "Aren't you supposed to do this on your own? Isn't that the entire idea?"

"Just for the first bit," she answered. "While I get settled into this whole thing."

"Don't tell me you're scared," he teased.

Grace swallowed. "A little," she answered. "I haven't been on my own for some time."

"I'm a stranger," the wolf reminded her.

She looked back at the trail again and felt her hands tremble slightly. Just the day before, he'd been the one convincing her that he was safe to keep around. Now, she was the one trying to convince him to stay.

"Ease me into it," she said again. "Besides, I was enjoying our conversation."

"That's because I was agreeing with you," the wolf said. "Everybody loves to hear that they're right."

Her backpack was still neatly waiting for her on the back seat, and she glanced at it.

"Please?" she begged, one last effort for company.

The wolf sighed. "Just a little while," he agreed. "Then you need to do this journey thing of yours. I'm rather keen to see how it ends."

Relief flooded her, crashing through her as she reached for her backpack. Already, the entrance to the trail seemed friendlier.

"Thank you," she whispered.

The wolf shrugged. "I grew up around these parts. It might be nice to experience some of it through the eyes of someone new."

THE CLIMB

Sweat clung to Grace's skin as she gave the wolf a sideways glance. He was covered in fur—might as well have been wrapped in blankets—but he seemed as cool as ever. His tongue, however, hung long out of the side of his mouth, drops of spit dripping every few seconds.

Grace had never been allowed a pet as a child. She had no idea what dogs were like, other than the smiling faces of those she'd met at her friend's houses. Judging by the wolf who walked beside her, they were not as they seemed.

It wasn't difficult to know that he was significantly fitter than she was. He showed little sign of burning lungs or aching knees. Instead, his eyes burned with an eagerness for what would come next, what would be waiting for them around the bends.

She did her best to hide her struggling breaths as she crawled up the mountainside. Already, she'd finished off half her water and most of her snacks.

The problem wasn't the hike itself. It was that they'd lost their way somewhere between their discussion about human belief and the effects of sunlight on the health of their hair.

"I thought you knew the way," Grace said, leaning against a rock. "You *said* that you know the way."

It was no use to try and hide it. She could no longer hide her exhaustion. It was clear in the redness of her cheeks and the shake that she felt in her knees.

"We should have been nearly there by now," she said.

"I thought I knew the way better than this," the wolf said. "I've only traversed this mountaintop a hundred times already. It looks a little different now."

"It can't be that different," she answered.

Her patience was wearing thin. The sun hung low in the sky, and soon the air would start to cool. If they didn't know their way up, they also didn't know their way down. They'd taken so many detours, each with the promise of landing them on the right path again, that she couldn't even be sure which side of the mountain they'd started their ascent on.

"I didn't bring a flashlight," she confessed.

The wolf offered her an amused smirk. "Not very prepared then."

"I wasn't expecting to be walking in the dark," she argued. "I should have just done this alone."

"Hey, I'm not the one who made you veer from your plan," he answered.

The wolf sat, his tail laid flat out behind him, his front paws tucked in front of his hind paws. Even seated, he was massive. She wondered for a moment if he'd like it if she reached out and stroked his head. Then again, they didn't know each other well enough for that.

So, she tucked her hands into her pockets to stop the temptation.

"I should have just stuck to the plan," she said. "I have the map with the trail all marked out. I would have been fine."

"If you have the map, then why were you following me?" he asked mid-lick of his paw.

"Because you said you knew the way and I assumed you would lead me down the right paths," she said.

He ignored that last statement. Stress started to tug at the muscles between her shoulders, and already she had a sense of the knots forming. It would take at least three Thai massages to work those out.

Why had she gone on that journey? On the mountain, with dark descending and her aching feet, she no longer saw the point of it at all.

"I'm sorry," she said. "This isn't your fault. I suppose I really don't know what I'm doing here."

The wolf paused. "Surely you're not giving up on this already?"

"Well, I don't have that choice. I'm already here. I just wish it had happened differently. It's going to be dark soon and I'm afraid," she said.

The words came with such ease, despite her confessing a state of mind that made her feel most vulnerable. Fear was something she let nobody see in her, and now, in the company of a stranger, a beast so unusual that she wasn't convinced he was real, she confessed it freely.

"I can see well at night," he said. "We can keep moving, and I can be your guide. There is no need to be afraid."

"Alright," she said. "Then let's keep moving. I'd really like to be in my bed tonight."

The wolf rose, stretched, and looked in one direction. He sniffed the air, as if to find his place, and then started walking.

"Stay close," he said. "Don't worry. I won't let you down again."

"You didn't let me down," she said with a sigh. "This just isn't what I thought it was."

"It hardly ever is," the wolf mumbled.

The road was rough and rocky. Despite his guidance, it made no difference to her failing night vision. The moon and stars had been covered up by thick clouds, making it a night darker than she'd known in some time. Those were no conditions for rookie mountaineering.

After the hundredth time that she stubbed her toe and hurled profanities at a meaningless rock, the wolf stopped and turned back toward her.

"Let me carry you," he said.

"What?" Grace recoiled, pulling herself away from him.

She hadn't meant her disgust; it was just that the offer had come so suddenly and felt so strange that it seemed absurd to accept it.

"I still have much energy left. I'm strong enough to do it, and you're starting to become a hazard to us both," he said. "It's really no problem. I'll drop to all fours, and you can rest a while on my back."

"I'm not sure that's a good idea," she said. "I'm not as light as I look."

"Don't be ridiculous," he said. "Besides, there are some more dangerous parts up ahead. The side of the path meets the edge of a cliff, and if you trip, you will most certainly die."

Grace swallowed. She looked around as if she would be able to spot an alternative option, as if suddenly her eyesight would come to life and she'd be more capable than she'd been their entire trip.

"O-okay," she said nervously.

The wolf dropped, just as he said he would, his front paws landing with a thud against the cold ground. She wasn't sure what to do. What was the proper way to mount a wolf?

His ears flicked, as if waiting impatiently for her as she tried to figure it out. Her feet burned, and her shoulders ached where her bag straps tugged at the skin.

"Whenever you're ready," the wolf said in his low, smooth voice.

She did the best she could, swinging one leg over his back as she weaved her fingers into his fur.

"Don't fall off," he warned. "And if you fall, please let go. I don't want to fall down this mountain with you. This is your journey, not mine."

"Got it," she said.

He took his first step, and she was certain that his legs would buckle beneath her weight. She tightened her core as she tried to keep her balance without pulling on his fur. She held on tight, though.

Grace had never even ridden a horse before. She had no idea where to put her feet or how to move along with him. She couldn't even be sure if she was supposed to lean forward or straighten her back.

"Grace," the wolf said, turning his head slightly backward.

"Mhmm?"

"You're crushing me with your thighs," he said. "You don't need to hold on so tight. I won't drop you."

"Oh, sorry," she mumbled.

She hadn't even realized it, but she'd been so worried about the rest of her, she hadn't noticed her thighs slowly pinching his ribs, increasing in strength the more worried she became about the road ahead.

"Are we at the scary part yet?" she asked.

"Not yet," he answered. "Would you like me to let you know when we're there?"

"No," she answered quickly. "I think I'd rather not know that I'm close to death."

They carried on largely in silence then. Grace focused on the brush of the cold air against her skin and the tightness of her grip. The wolf's fur was softer than it looked, and much thicker.

She'd reach in as deep as she could to hold on, until the tips of her fingers had brushed his skin. His fur covered her hands, with just the ends of her wrists sticking out. How had he survived the heat?

Although now that it was dark and much colder, she envied his coat. She hadn't prepared for nighttime, and so, soon enough, her lips and nose were numb.

It was meant to be an uplifting journey. She'd dreamed of reaching the top of the mountain, looking out at the view, and accepting that she was a new woman with a new life and fresh boundaries.

Instead, she wished rather to get home as quickly as possible so that she could crawl beneath the covers, put on her favorite show, and order the same takeout she ordered every week. She was too far away from her comfort routine and utterly filled with regret.

"How much further?" she asked.

The wolf stopped. "Much," he answered. "And I'm afraid that I am growing rather tired."

"Let's rest," she offered, sliding from his back.

He was quick to sit, and she saw then the droop of his head. Grace sat next to him in the dark. She could make out a few bushes and a nearby rock. She could also tell they were beneath a tree, but there was little more than that for her in that world.

"Thank you for carrying me," she said. "I think I can walk the rest of the way again now."

"You might be able to," he said. "But I don't know if I can. I need a moment to sleep and regain some energy."

Her stomach twisted. "But I don't know where I am," she said. "I can't find my way without you."

"Then you will have to wait for me," he said. "I've not had a drink from a stream in some time, and this has been a long day without sleep for a creature like me."

She reached for her bottle and bowl and poured out some water for him, which he'd lapped up happily. Grace remembered her friend's boxer. He'd slept often in the day, and she wondered if it was the same for wolves.

"Get some rest," she said, uncertain of how eager she was for it.

"Thank you," the wolf answered. "I'll be ready to carry on soon enough."

He lay down, and suddenly, she felt all alone. There was no barrier between her and the wind, no conversation to keep her mind quiet. It was just her and the world, and that was too much to manage.

She heard as his breathing grew slower, louder even. In the dark, she could just make out his shape, his body heaving with every breath. Her body screamed with exhaustion. She was hungry and tired and fed up with the mountain she was on.

Grace curled up beside the wolf, the cold of the ground beneath her a jarring sensation to her skin. It felt like torture, the breeze curling over her skin, creeping into her clothes and her ears, brushing her hair across her face. She couldn't close the window; she couldn't pull the covers over her ears. But as she turned to make herself comfortable, she found herself tangled in his fur.

It was as good a blanket as any, and with the shelter from the cold and wind, her eyes grew heavy, and she drifted off to sleep.

THE PEAK

SHE WAS WARM, AND her breathing heavy. The rock beneath her no longer hurt or bothered her. In fact, most of the right side of her body had gone numb. Her slumber had become something rhythmic, guided by the ebb and flow of the beast in which she was wrapped.

It had been some time since Grace had fallen asleep so easily and dreamed of nothing at all. The feeling was about as good as a holiday.

Sun burned against her hand, her fingers outstretched beyond the wolf's fur. Grace blinked a few times, struggling to make sense of the world around her. She could see just a sliver of light through the grey of his fur. Against her back, she could feel the wolf's heavy breathing. He was still asleep.

She parted the fur that covered just about all of her and looked out. It was a bright morning. They'd slept through whatever was left of the night.

When she sat up, she struggled to understand any of it. Her movement stirred the wolf. He let out a huff, and he stretched his legs out straight around her.

The view was remarkable. There was nothing but sky around her, with the rest of the world down below. Birds tweeted and chattered as she took her first yawn.

"We're at the peak," she said in disbelief.

The wolf licked his lips a few times and blinked as he sat up beside her.

"Oh yes, I thought it would be a nice surprise for you," he said. "I knew that it meant a lot."

"You planned this?" she asked.

"Are you angry about it?" he countered.

How she was meant to feel was a mystery to her. Grace rose to her feet and took a few careful steps. They burned from the walk the day before. As did her legs and shoulders.

"Will you carry me back down?" she asked, fixated on the rising sun.

"Sure," he answered.

"Then I'm not angry," she said.

There had been such certainty the night before that all had been lost, that she would never get to the peak and see the view. Rather, she'd anticipated further nighttime walking, a late drive back to her accommodation, a vending machine dinner, and a frustrated night's sleep.

The rock beneath her warmed from the sun as she took another careful step forward.

"Easy," the wolf said with a chuckle. "I didn't bring you all the way up here just to watch you fall off."

She was here! It was time for her to decide who she wanted to be, to know what the world meant to her, and what she wanted from it in return. That was the moment she'd been after, so that she could move on from all that had gone wrong in her past.

However, now that it was here, she didn't know what she thought or felt. Was it because she hadn't done it on her own? Was it because she hadn't expected it?

"This view never gets old," the wolf said. "I'm glad we made it up here."

"Thank you for coming with me," Grace said. "This has truly been the adventure of a lifetime."

It no longer mattered how strange he had been, or why he had chosen to speak to her on her first night there. All that mattered was that he'd listened and done for her what she'd needed him to.

"I don't believe it," she whispered to herself.

The hunger that burned in her stomach no longer mattered. She wasn't alone, and still she felt as free as ever.

She turned to catch him stretching. He arched his back and then raised his hind legs so that they were straight.

"Why did you help me?" she asked.

He licked his lips a few times and sighed. "I had nothing else to do. There's not much for someone like me in these parts."

"Thank you," she said.

"I felt bad," he confessed. "You were so upset with me last night for getting us lost. I thought about how much this journey is supposed to mean to you and, while I don't quite get it, I felt that I had ruined it."

She shook her head. "It isn't your fault," she said. "I had a map, and I never checked it. You've done more than you needed to."

"I'm glad we're at the top." He glanced over her shoulder at the view behind her. "And it's good to see you feeling so positive about things again."

A rush of air crawled up the side of the mountain and over her skin. Grace closed her eyes to greet it as it washed through her hair.

Everything was going to be alright. She was certain of it.

"I'm afraid you won't have much time up here," the wolf said. "Enjoy the view while you can."

Turning from him again, she tried to focus on the details. Below, she could just make out the roads of the village. Other hiking paths decorated the surrounding hills and mountain tops. Somewhere in the distance, a predator bird called, and she searched for a sign of it.

"Tell me, Grace," the wolf said, coming up behind her. "Did you get what you were hoping for on this journey?"

Reaching deep for the answer, she did her best to make it what it was meant to be. But that just wasn't the case.

"No," she said. "I didn't. I got something else perhaps, but I feel no closer to knowing who I am or what I want from this world."

"That's a pity," he answered. "I was really hoping to find that out. I'll admit, it interested me a little."

Did wolves struggle with marriage and divorce? It occurred to her then that her problems must have seemed so foreign to him, so strange and unnecessary. All that effort she'd made to start her journey at The Crag, and now she was confronted with the triviality of it all.

"Maybe it will come to me on the way down," she said, hopeful. "Either way, I'm pleased to be here."

"It wasn't a wasted effort, then?" he asked.

"Certainly not."

The sound of cicadas burst through the air, a sign that all life had woken and that the world was in motion once more. Grace took a deep breath, holding in for a moment before letting it out slowly.

A cup of coffee would have been good. A bite of breakfast, perhaps. The wolf was right: they couldn't stay there long. She'd gone too long without eating and so had he. There was still the entire journey down the mountain.

It was embarrassment that crept into her reality then. It dawned on Grace that she'd asked too much of the wolf. He'd starved and exhausted himself for her, and it had been a pointless endeavor. She was no nearer to her resolve.

How much did that truly matter? If she made it back home with no further answers, at least she knew one thing for certain. The world was not nearly as tedious as she once believed it to be.

There were great wolves that sat down at restaurant tables. She had ridden on his back and slept between his fur. While she doubted most people would believe her, it didn't bother her much. Grace knew it to be true, and it gave her hope for the life that was still left for her.

Maybe she could change and find freedom where she needed it most. After all, she'd spent the night pressed against the belly of a wolf and lived to tell the tale.

How much of her sentimental thought would mean anything to him, she couldn't be sure. After all, she'd had to practically beg him to come up the mountain with her in the first place.

Guilt followed embarrassment. He hadn't wanted to do it. The wolf wanted to go home and spend a quiet day in his own company. Instead, he'd fought part of her battle for her.

"I'm sorry," she said. "This is more than you signed up for. You were only supposed to give me directions to the start of the trail."

He raised his hind leg to scratch behind his ear. "Please, this is sort of how I roll, I guess," he said. "I'm a go-with-the-flow kind of guy."

"I should be more like that," Grace confessed. "I was perfectly prepared to abandon my efforts yesterday, all just because we got a little bit lost."

"We got very lost," he reminded her.

"That's not the point." Grace turned back toward the sun, as if to speak directly into the landscape ahead of her. "I shouldn't forget my goals. I should approach life the way you do. I should let go of the journey and know that the goal is inevitable as long as I keep going."

"I suppose," the wolf said. "That's not what I meant by all this, by the way, but I'm glad you've learned something from it."

She wished to sit there forever, until starvation set in and she drifted into a long sleep again. The thought of returning to a world with office hours and deadlines seemed absurd to her. Let alone the abomination of traffic lights.

Distance was what she'd needed all along, and he had offered her that. He'd shown her something she hadn't known was missing, and he'd done so with such ease and charm that, now that she was there, it felt as if it had been planned all along.

The world fell silent around them. It was so instant that it sent a ripple of discomfort through Grace. There was no sound of bird calls in the sky, and no clicks and whines of the cicadas.

The air felt thick then, and her heart started to heave heavier in her chest. Grace tried to explain it away. She was exhausted, hungry, and overly excited. Whichever word she could think of, she clung to as a reason for her sudden change in disposition.

It made her dizzy, uneasy in her place. What had caused their sudden pause? It was as if the living world around her had scampered. Whatever they knew, she had missed it. Perhaps the wolf had noticed.

Grace turned just in time to see the white flash of fangs. There was no chance to fight. Her skin popped as they pierced through into her neck. She was nothing but a small figure beneath his tall and looming shape.

As quickly as she'd felt she had found life, she was losing it.

Grace knew then precisely who she was. She knew her boundaries, and he had crossed every one of them.

He tore at her, and she felt the flesh rip from her body. Piece by piece, he reduced her to nothing. She would become part of him then, and she would never make it back down that mountain.

Fragmented, her spirit searched for a reason.

The dinner, the drive, their ascent, all to culminate in one massive loss.

In the end, the answer was simple. It was hidden in his belly, right at the core of the wolf where only those most unfortunate could find it.

He was hungry and she was there.

THANK YOU

Thank you for reading my novelette! Do *you* ever ignore red flags when meeting a charming stranger? Surely no one as strange as a talking wolf, but I wonder how much others trust those they don't know.

Speaking of which... Can I trust you to leave a review? I'd be thrilled to hear your thoughts on my story if you have a spare minute. Reviews help me hone my storytelling and help other potential readers find my books. You can leave one where you acquired the book, or at my publisher's website below. Sincerely, thank you!

https://hylosis.pub

ABOUT THE AUTHOR

https://hylosis.pub/pages/author-kat-goss

With a passion for exploring strange ideas and reimagining normal situations through an alternative lens, Kat Goss crafts stories that challenge perceptions and keep readers involved. Away from her screen, Kat enjoys unraveling the complexities of human nature and searching for the unusual in the usual.

Kat lives in Stanford, a heritage village in South Africa where she lives a quiet life with her wife and a small menagerie of animals. When she isn't writing, she spends her time traveling and cooking.

ALSO BY THE AUTHOR

https://hylosis.pub/products/the-client

One missing person. Two tangled lives. Freelance editor Natalie innocently replies to an email about her missing client, only to find herself ensnared in a web that threatens to destroy her career, her marriage, and her life.

The Client is a domestic psychological thriller and Kat Goss's inspiration for this novelette.

Available wide. Get a discount on digital formats (eBook and audiobook) on Hylosis Publishing with code:

GATWCLIENT

ABOUT THE PUBLISHER

https://hylosis.pub/pages/publishing

Hylosis Publishing is an independent publisher located in Chandler, Arizona. We firmly believe everyone has a story to tell or a unique perspective to share. We're always on the lookout for talented thinkers and storytellers.

Interested in getting published? Apply using the link above.

www.ingramcontent.com/pod-product-compliance
Lightning Source LLC
Chambersburg PA
CBHW030013010826
48973CB00009B/2782